Karate Katie

by Nancy Krulik • illustrated by John & Wendy

Grosset & Dunlap

For Ian: my favorite second-
dan black belt!—N.K.

For Erik S.: a black belt
on the drums—J&W

GROSSET & DUNLAP
Published by the Penguin Group
Penguin Group (USA) Inc., 375 Hudson Street,
New York, New York 10014, U.S.A.
Penguin Group (Canada), 90 Eglinton Avenue East, Suite 700,
Toronto, Ontario, Canada M4P 2Y3
(a division of Pearson Penguin Canada Inc.)
Penguin Books Ltd, 80 Strand, London WC2R 0RL, England
Penguin Ireland, 25 St Stephen's Green, Dublin 2, Ireland
(a division of Penguin Books Ltd)
Penguin Group (Australia), 250 Camberwell Road,
Camberwell, Victoria 3124, Australia
(a division of Pearson Australia Group Pty Ltd)
Penguin Books India Pvt Ltd, 11 Community Centre,
Panchsheel Park, New Delhi - 110 017, India
Penguin Group (NZ), Cnr Airborne and Rosedale Roads,
Albany, Auckland 1310, New Zealand
(a division of Pearson New Zealand Ltd)
Penguin Books (South Africa) (Pty) Ltd, 24 Sturdee Avenue,
Rosebank, Johannesburg 2196, South Africa

Penguin Books Ltd, Registered Offices:
80 Strand, London WC2R 0RL, England

Text copyright © 2006 by Nancy Krulik. Illustrations copyright © 2006 by
John and Wendy. All rights reserved. Published by Grosset & Dunlap, a
division of Penguin Young Readers Group, 345 Hudson Street, New York,
New York 10014. GROSSET & DUNLAP is a trademark of Penguin Group
(USA) Inc. Printed in the U.S.A.

Library of Congress Control Number: 2005013424

ISBN 0-448-43767-8   10 9 8 7 6 5

Chapter 1

"Hey, George, wait up!" Katie Carew called out as she ran toward her pal, George Brennan.

Like Katie, George was dressed in his red and white Cherrydale Elementary School T-shirt. He also wore a pair of white shorts and sneakers. That was their track team uniform.

"Hurry up, Katie Kazoo," he answered, using the special nickname he had made up for her. "We can't be late for the track meet."

"I'm coming!" Katie hurried faster toward George.

But instead of waiting for her, George began to run. "Last one to the field is a rotten egg!" he shouted.

"George, wait! Your sneaker's untie—"

Before Katie could even finish the word, George tripped over his shoelace. He fell face-down into the dirt.

"Nice one," Evan, one of the fifth-graders on the track team, teased as he ran past.

George blushed as he sat up. He didn't say anything while he tied his shoelace.

Just then, Kevin Camilleri, George's best friend, came walking over.

"What are you doing down there?" Kevin asked George. "Aren't you going to the track meet this afternoon? You'd better get over to the field."

George looked up at his best friend. "How about you?" he asked Kevin. "The meet starts in a few minutes. Why aren't you in your uniform?"

Katie had been wondering the same thing.

Kevin was on the track team just like she and George were. But instead of his team T-shirt and shorts, Kevin was wearing his white karate uniform. He had a bright yellow belt around his waist.

"You can't run dressed like that," George said. "Coach Debbie's going to be so angry when she sees you."

"I'm not going to the track meet," Kevin told him.

"But you *have* to," Katie interrupted. "Everyone on the team is supposed to be there."

"I'm not on the team anymore," Kevin told them. "I gave Coach Debbie a note from my mom this morning."

"You quit the team?" Katie couldn't believe her ears.

Kevin nodded. "I had to. My karate class is on Tuesdays and Thursdays. The track meets are on Thursdays. I couldn't do both. So I picked karate."

George jumped up. "Well, un-pick it!" he exclaimed. "You and I are supposed to run in the relay race today."

Katie looked over at George. His face was all red. He sounded really angry. Not that Katie blamed him. George had really been looking forward to running in the relay race with Kevin.

But Kevin didn't seem to care. "So what?" he asked with a shrug. "You can still run. Coach Debbie will just put someone else in for me."

George shook his head. "That's not the point!" he declared. "We've been practicing for weeks. We have the baton handoff down per-fectly."

"Sorry, dude," Kevin said. "But I have karate today! This is my first class as a yellow belt. I just passed the promotion test last week. Boy, was it hard. I had to learn all these new forms, and break two pieces of wood!"

Katie watched as Kevin fingered his bright

yellow belt. He was obviously very proud of having earned it.

"Big deal," George moaned. "A yellow belt. Yellow like chicken feathers. That's perfect. You're a chicken, too. You're chickening out of the race."

"Am not!" Kevin shouted.

"Are too!" George shouted back.

Just then, a car horn started beeping.

Kevin's mom had arrived. "Hurry up, Kevin," Mrs. Camilleri shouted. "You don't want to be late for karate."

"I sure don't!" Kevin agreed. He turned and ran over to the car without even saying good-bye to George and Katie.

"I can't believe he did this to me," George said to Katie as the car pulled away.

Katie felt really bad for George. "Come on," she urged him. "You're going to be great, even without Kevin."

George shook his head. "I doubt it," he said. But he turned and followed her to the field anyway. Kevin may have been a quitter. But George sure wasn't.

Chapter 2

Most of the kids on the team were already warming up when Katie and George reached the field.

Jeremy Fox was busy stretching on the ground. He looked up and smiled. "Hey, Katie," he said. "Are you ready for the meet?"

Katie nodded. "I think so. I'm doing the long jump today."

"Awesome!" Jeremy exclaimed. "That's your best event. You jumped really far during the last practice." He glanced over at George, who had a very angry look on his face. "What's wrong with you?" Jeremy asked.

"*Grrrr*," George growled.

"He's mad because Kevin quit the track team. Now he has to run the relay race with someone else," Katie explained.

"Oh," Jeremy said. "That stinks."

"*Grrrr,*" George growled again.

Just then, Katie heard someone call her name from across the field.

"Hi, Katie!" Suzanne Lock shouted.

Katie laughed when she saw what Suzanne was wearing. Suzanne always managed to make her uniform look just a little bit different from everyone else's. Today she was wearing red and white ribbons in her hair. She had also used fabric paint to draw a red cherry on the sleeve of her T-shirt.

"Hey, Suzanne," Katie greeted her. "Nice shirt."

"Thanks," Suzanne said. "The cherry is for Cherrydale Elementary School."

"Coach Debbie's not going to like it," Jeremy told Suzanne. "She wants all of our uniforms to look the same."

"I never look the same as anyone else," Suzanne told him.

Katie had to agree with that. Suzanne was definitely different.

"*Grrr,*" George growled again. He was even too angry to make a joke about the cherry that was painted on Suzanne's shirt.

"What's with him?" Suzanne asked.

"Kevin quit the track team," Katie explained.

"Oh. You just found out. I knew about that *yesterday*," Suzanne boasted. "Kevin's mother told my mother that he likes karate class better. That's why he quit."

"But he made a promise to be part of the track team," George told her. "You don't just break a promise. Now I have to run the relay without him."

"Oh, big deal," Suzanne said. "You can run with someone else."

"It's not the same," George moaned.

Suzanne shook her head. "You whine just like my baby sister," she told him.

Katie gulped. This was getting ugly. Suzanne got on George's nerves even when he was in a good mood. And today, George was in a bad mood. There was no way he was going to put up with Suzanne being mean to him.

"I wish you would just shut up!" George shouted at Suzanne. "Forever!"

Katie gasped. George had just made a wish. *A really mean wish*. George had done a terrible thing.

But Katie couldn't really be angry with him. George hadn't known what he was doing when he said that. He was just screaming because he was angry. He had no idea about the power of wishes.

How could he? Katie hadn't known about it, either—until the day the magic wind came along.

It had all started one really bad day last year when Katie was in third grade. She'd had a terrible day. She'd lost the football game for her team, gotten mud all over her favorite pants, and burped really loud in front of the whole class.

That night, Katie wished she could be anyone other than herself.

There must have been a shooting star overhead when she made that wish, because the very next day the magic wind came. It turned Katie into Speedy, the hamster in her third-grade classroom! Katie spent the whole morning going around and around on a hamster wheel and gnawing on chew sticks!

The magic wind came back again and again after that. Sometimes it changed Katie into other kids, like Jeremy, Suzanne, and even Suzanne's baby sister, Heather.

Other times it turned her into adults—like Cinnamon, the woman who owned the candy store in the Cherrydale Mall. What a mess *that* had been! Katie had accidentally sent candy hearts with mean messages to some of her friends at school. She'd almost ruined Valentine's Day forever!

Another time the magic wind had turned Katie into Lucille, the lunch lady in the school cafeteria. That time, Katie had started a food fight and gotten Lucille fired. It took all the kids in school to get her hired back again.

In fact, it seemed like Katie got into trouble whenever the magic wind came. And so did the person she turned into. That was why Katie didn't like wishes. When they came true, they really could make a mess of things!

Chapter 3

"Go, Emma, go!" Katie shouted as the relay race began. Coach Debbie had put Emma Weber in as George's partner in the race. Now Emma W. was running as fast as she could down the track. She held a metal baton in her hand as she ran.

Katie really cheered her two pals on! "Come on, Emma!" she shouted loudly.

Emma W. was running pretty fast. She was tied with the runner from the other team. As Emma reached the finish line, she handed the white baton over to George. He took off and ran down the track.

"Come on, George!" Katie yelled. "You can

do it!" She really wanted her team to win.

"Move it, George!" Suzanne screamed toward the field. "Go faster! FASTER!"

Unfortunately, George wasn't moving very fast at all. He hadn't tied his shoelace very well. It came untied when he started to run. Now his sneaker kept falling off his foot.

A few moments later, a runner for the other team crossed the finish line. George was way behind.

As George crossed the finish line, Emma W. and Katie were there waiting for him.

"It's okay," Emma told George. "We'll get them next time."

"*Grrr!*" George growled. "There won't be any next time."

Katie shook her head. "Come on, George. That's not fair. It's not Emma's fault you lost the race."

"No. It's Kevin's fault," George grumbled. "I hate him."

Katie shook her head. She knew it wasn't

Kevin's fault at all. If George had just tied his shoelace, he might have had a chance.

But there was no sense telling George that now. He wasn't going to listen anyway.

"Katie, it's almost time for the long jump," Coach Debbie called out. "You'd better start warming up."

"Okay," Katie called back.

"Good luck," Suzanne told her.

Katie looked at Suzanne strangely. Her voice sounded kind of hoarse. *Uh-oh! What if George's mean wish was coming true?*

"Are you okay?" she asked Suzanne.

Suzanne nodded. "Sure, I'm fine. I've just got a sore throat. It's my third one this month."

"Are you sure?" Katie asked her.

"Stop worrying about me," Suzanne continued. "Worry about how you're going to beat that girl from Oakwood Elementary School in the long jump. Have you seen how tall she is?"

Suzanne wasn't kidding. The girl from Oakwood Elementary had really long legs. And, boy, could she jump! Still, Katie had come in second place against the four people who were jumping. That was the best she'd ever placed in a track meet.

"I think I did pretty well," Katie told Suzanne that night while the two girls were on the phone.

"You did," Suzanne assured her. "But no matter how you did, you would have been better than George. What a klutz."

"Why are you so mean to him?" Katie asked her.

"*I'm* mean?" Suzanne insisted. She coughed hoarsely. "How about him? Did you hear what he said to me?"

Katie sighed. How could she forget?

"Besides, he's always blaming other people for his—" Suzanne stopped in the middle of her sentence and began coughing again.

"Are you okay?" Katie asked her.

Suzanne coughed harder. When she finally stopped, there was silence on her end of the phone.

"Suzanne?" Katie asked. "Are you there?"

The answer came back in a hoarse whisper. "I think I lost my voice," Suzanne struggled to say.

Katie gasped. George's wish had come true!

Chapter 4

Katie didn't sleep very well that night. She was really worried about Suzanne. What if she *never* got her voice back? How would she sing along with Bayside Boys songs? Or answer questions in school? Or talk on the phone? And what would Suzanne be like if she couldn't brag all the time?

It was hard to believe. Katie really would miss hearing Suzanne's boasting.

✕ ✕ ✕

When Katie arrived at school the next morning, she spotted Suzanne across the school yard. A group of fourth-grade girls were standing around her. Katie rushed over to her friend. She hoped she was all right.

"How are you?" Katie asked Suzanne.

Suzanne picked up a pink heart-shaped pad. She used a bright purple pen to write a message on it.

I just lost my voice, she wrote. *No problem*.

But Katie knew Suzanne was wrong. She had a big problem. Bigger than she knew.

"I like that pen," Emma Stavros said. "I have a green one just like it."

Suzanne rolled her eyes. *Purple is prettier*, she wrote.

"Your mom said you could come to school with a sore throat?" Katie asked, amazed. Mrs. Carew would never have let Katie come to school if she were sick.

Sure, Suzanne wrote on her pad. *My mom called the doctor. He said it wasn't catching. It is okay for me to be here, as long as I don't talk.*

"*KEEYAH!*"

Suddenly, Katie heard a loud scream. She quickly turned to see what had happened. Across the yard she saw Kevin. He was lifting his leg and kicking at the air.

"*KEEYAH!*" Kevin shouted again as he kicked even harder.

"What's he doing?" Miriam Chan asked.

"I think that's karate," Mandy Banks told her. "It's all Kevin thinks about these days."

Katie watched as a group of boys walked over to Kevin. George was one of them. He did not look happy. He still looked really angry with Kevin.

George was going to start an argument with Kevin. Katie just knew it. He might even make another mean wish.

Katie couldn't let something horrible happen to someone else just because of George's temper! She had to stop him!

"I'll be right back," Katie told Suzanne and the others.

Quickly, she hurried over to where the

boys were. "Hi, George," she greeted him. "Did you do the math homework? Can I see what answer you got for number three?"

Katie was trying to turn George's attention from Kevin. But it wasn't working.

"In a minute, Katie Kazoo," George replied. "I'm watching the kung fu fool."

"It's karate, not kung fu," Kevin told him.

"And *you're* the fool."

"I'm not the one kicking the air," George said. "Are you trying to break wind?"

The boys laughed.

"Break wind! Good one, George," Manny Gonzalez said.

"I'm doing a flying side kick," Kevin told him. "You have to know how to do one to be a yellow belt."

George rolled his eyes. "Whatever," he said.

"The flying side kick is a good way to break a wooden board," Kevin continued. "In fact, that's how I'm going to break the board in my karate competition this weekend."

"You're going to be in a competition?" Jeremy asked. He sounded really impressed.

Kevin nodded. "Uh-huh. It's on Sunday. I'm competing against other yellow belts."

"You're going to beat them up?" Kadeem Carter asked excitedly.

"It's called *sparring*," Kevin corrected him. "And you wear a lot of padding and a helmet.

So no one actually gets hurt."

"Oh." Kadeem didn't sound so excited anymore.

"But I'm going to break a wooden board, too," Kevin told him. "And I'm going to do a few karate forms."

"That sounds really neat," Katie said.

"It sounds really dumb," George muttered.

"*You're* dumb," Kevin shouted back.

"No way! *You* are," George argued loudly.

Katie pulled on the straps of George's backpack. "Come on, George," she said. "Show me how to do that math problem."

"Fine," George said with a huff. "I don't feel like listening to Karate Kevin anymore, anyway. He's such a bragger! I can't stand him!"

Katie sighed. She didn't know whether Kevin could use karate to break a piece of wood. But he'd sure used it to break up his friendship with George.

Chapter 5

At lunchtime, Katie sat down at a table beside Suzanne. Emma W. and Jessica Haynes sat across from them.

"How's your throat?" Emma W. asked Suzanne.

Suzanne picked up her purple pen. *It hurts a little*, she wrote.

"Ms. Sweet has been so nice to Suzanne," Jessica told the girls. "She said that since Suzanne couldn't talk, she is going to teach us how to spell in American Sign Language. It's the language some deaf people use to talk to each other. Ms. Sweet has a chart that shows us how to make all the letters with our hands."

"That's cool," Emma W. said. "Maybe you could teach Katie and me how to do sign language, too. We can all sign to one another. It will be like our secret code!"

Suzanne scribbled a new note on her pad. *It won't be too secret. The kids in our class are all learning how to do it. Of course, no one else in your class will, so it could be your secret.*

Katie laughed. Suzanne had figured out a way to brag, after all.

As Katie took a bite of her peanut butter sandwich, she looked over at the next table. Kevin was sitting there with Manny and Jeremy. He was throwing cherry tomatoes up in the air and catching them with his mouth.

Usually, George would be sitting next to Kevin. But today, George was at another table, with Kadeem and Andrew.

Of course, that didn't mean George couldn't hear what Kevin was saying at his table. Everybody could hear Kevin. He was talking really loudly.

"My karate teacher said I should break a thin board at the competition," Kevin said between tomatoes. "But I told him, 'No way!' Why should I take the easy way out? I can break a thick board. I'm really strong."

"Isn't that kind of dangerous?" Jeremy asked him. "You could hurt your foot or something."

"Not if you know how to do it right," Kevin boasted. "And *I* know how. But my teacher is still making me break a thin board."

"Hey, Kevin," Kadeem called out. "Why did the Karate Kid cross the road?"

"Why?" Kevin asked.

"To break the board on the other side," Kadeem answered. He chuckled at his own joke.

George wasn't about to let Kadeem have the last laugh. "What do you get when you mix a blue belt and a black belt?" he shouted out.

"What?" Jeremy asked.

"A bruise belt!" George laughed. "Get it? You get all black and blue!"

Kevin rolled his eyes. "That would never happen, George," he said. "In a tournament, you spar with kids who are at the same level you are. I'll be sparring with other yellow belts. Of course, I'm going to be better than they are."

Uh-oh. Katie knew George was going to be angry at Kevin for ruining his joke. George took his joking very seriously.

Just then, George leaped up from his seat. He began to wave his arms and legs around wildly. *"YAHHHHH!"* he shouted. He stuck his tongue out and made a goofy face. "Look at me! I'm Karate Kevin."

All the kids started to laugh.

"You're just jealous, George!" Kevin shouted. "I'm going to be the champion of this tournament. *You* never win at anything. I heard what happened at that track meet. Everybody did."

Wow! Katie couldn't believe Kevin had just said that. It was really mean.

"That's not true," Katie said, defending George. "He wins at joke-offs all the time."

"Hey!" Kadeem argued. "I win some of those, too."

"I know," Katie admitted. She knew that when it came to class 4A's joke competitions, George and Kadeem were both really funny. "But George also wins sometimes," Katie continued. "So Kevin was wrong."

"Maybe I'm wrong," Kevin told

her. "But I'm also *strong*!" He jumped up and kicked his leg, karate-style.

"Stop bragging," Katie warned him. "It's not nice."

"Yeah," Jeremy agreed. "Besides, we don't have time to talk about karate anymore. We only have a half-hour recess after lunch today. And we're going to play soccer, remember?"

"It's 4A against 4B," Kadeem added.

"I don't have time for soccer," Kevin said, sounding very stuck-up. "I have to practice my karate forms during recess."

"But you have to play," Mandy reminded him. "You're our goalie."

"Let someone else play goalie," Kevin suggested.

"You're *always* goalie," Mandy reminded him. "No one else has had any practice at it."

"We planned this game two days ago," Kadeem said angrily. "How come you waited until today to tell us you didn't want to play?"

"Yeah," Andrew Epstein agreed. "If you

had told us earlier, then someone else could have practiced being goalie."

"Sorry," Kevin said. "I guess I didn't think about it."

"All you think about these days is karate," Emma S. told him.

"Karate is the most important thing in the world to me," Kevin explained.

Now *all* of the kids in class 4A were angry with Kevin. He was letting them down.

"We'll win anyway," Andrew assured Kadeem. "We don't need Karate Kevin."

"That's right," George agreed. He raised his leg and made a wobbly kick in the air. "We're kicking him off the team. Later for you, Karate Kevin."

Chapter 6

At the end of the school day, the kids in class 4A went home feeling awful. They had lost the soccer game at recess . . . badly. The score was seven to one. Everyone was blaming Kevin.

But Kevin didn't care. He stood on the steps of the school kicking his legs out, pretending to break wooden boards.

"You should be practicing catching soccer balls," Andrew told him. "That would have helped us today."

Kevin ignored him.

"I think Kevin's a secret weapon," Kadeem said.

"Are you nuts?" George asked. "We lost because of him."

"I meant he was a secret weapon for the *other* team!" Kadeem explained.

The other kids all laughed. Even Katie. Usually she hated it when her friends made fun of someone. But Kevin deserved it. He'd really let his team down . . . again.

Just then, Becky Stern, Jeremy Fox, and Jessica Haynes walked out of the school. They did not look sad. Why should they? *Their* class had won the soccer game.

"Where's Suzanne?" Katie asked Jessica. Usually, Jessica and Suzanne left school together.

"She went home after recess," Jessica explained. "She was coughing a lot. Ms. Sweet sent her to the nurse's office."

"Her mom picked her up and took her to the doctor," Becky continued.

"I hope she's not very sick. Maybe he can give her some medicine to bring her voice back," Emma W. suggested.

Katie doubted that. She was pretty sure the problem Suzanne had wasn't something that could be cured by a doctor.

✕ ✕ ✕

"You're awfully quiet tonight," Mrs. Carew said to Katie at dinnertime.

Katie shrugged and picked at the vegetarian lasagna on her plate. "I don't have anything to say."

"Did anything bad happen at school?" her mom asked.

"We lost a soccer game to class 4B," Katie told her.

"Is that all?" Katie's dad asked. "When I was in school, my team always lost. It never stopped me from eating."

Losing a soccer game wouldn't really keep Katie from eating, either. Actually, it was Suzanne that Katie was so upset about.

Brrring. Just then the phone rang.

"I'll get it," Katie said. She leaped up from

the table so fast, she almost tripped over Pepper, who had been sitting at her feet.

Mrs. Carew shook her head. "No. I'll get it. You keep eating."

Katie sat down and placed a forkful of lasagna in her mouth. Then she reached down and slipped a slippery lasagna noodle into Pepper's mouth. The grateful cocker spaniel chewed it up in no time.

"Oh, that's a shame," Katie heard her mother say. "Is Suzanne okay about it?"

Katie gulped. It must be Suzanne's mother on the phone. What awful news was she telling her? Was it that the doctor had said Suzanne would never speak again? That wasn't news. Katie already knew that.

"That was Mrs. Lock," Mrs. Carew told Katie as she sat back down at the dinner table. "Suzanne just got back from the doctor's office. She has another sore throat. And she can't talk, either."

"I know," Katie said. "She went home right

after recess. It's awful. George made that wish and . . ."

"George?" Mrs. Carew asked. "What does he have to do with anything?"

"Well, he made a wish that Suzanne would shut up and . . ." Katie began.

Mrs. Carew shook her head. "Katie, I assure you, this has nothing to do with an argument between Suzanne and George," she said. "Suzanne has a sore throat because her tonsils are infected. She's going to have an operation to have her tonsils taken out."

"Her tonsils?" Katie asked.

"Yes," Mrs. Carew said. "The doctor is operating tomorrow morning. She'll be in a little pain for a while, but then she'll be good as new."

"Suzanne's going to have an operation?" Katie asked. She was so relieved. "That's great!"

Her parents looked at her strangely.

"Great?" Mr. Carew asked, surprised.

39

Oops.

"I mean, it's great that she'll be able to talk again after her tonsils come out," Katie said. "You know how Suzanne loves to talk."

"Almost as much as I love to eat," Mr. Carew laughed. "Can I have some more lasagna, please?"

Katie giggled. Then she took a big bite of her own lasagna. Suddenly, she was hungry, too.

Chapter 7

"Pass five basil leaves, please," Becky Stern said.

"Here you go," Mandy Banks replied as she passed a bowl of fresh basil leaves across the counter in Katie's kitchen.

"Mmm . . ." Katie's mother sniffed at the air as she stirred the tomato sauce that was cooking in a pot on the stove. "I'm so glad you kids formed a cooking club. My house always smells so good on Saturdays."

"And *we* always eat well on Saturdays," George told her. "This tomato sauce is going to be awesome!"

"I know," Katie said. She looked down at

her cookbook. "We need to grind some fresh pepper."

Woof! Woof! Katie's dog barked at the sound of his name.

"No, silly," Katie giggled. "Not you."

"I can't believe Kevin is missing the cooking club meeting when we're making tomato sauce," Emma W. said as she peeled the skin from a juicy red tomato.

"He's probably practicing karate today," Jeremy said. "Karate's more important to him than anything."

"Even *tomatoes*?" Emma asked. She didn't sound so sure. Kevin loved tomatoes.

"Maybe Kevin just didn't want to be around us," Katie said quietly.

"Oh, come on. *We're* the ones who don't want to be around *him*," George replied.

"That's what I mean," Katie told him.

"Huh?" George asked.

"We were all kind of rotten to Kevin yesterday," Katie admitted.

"No way. He was rotten to us! He made us lose the soccer game! And he made me lose the relay race," George insisted.

Katie knew that it was George's loose shoelace that had made him lose that race. She also knew that having a different goalie wouldn't make a soccer team lose by six points. But she wasn't going to tell George that. He'd just argue with her about it anyway.

"Maybe we were *all* wrong," Katie said finally.

"We were kind of mean," Emma W. agreed.

"I guess we didn't have to keep calling him Karate Kevin," Jeremy added.

"He didn't have to keep bragging about being so strong," George argued back.

"Or being better than everyone else in his karate class," Becky said.

"No, he didn't. But we've all bragged before," Katie said. She turned to Becky. "Do you remember when you learned to do that backflip in gymnastics class? You talked about that for weeks."

Becky blushed. "Well, how about that time you taught Pepper how to roll over? All you kept saying was how smart your dog was."

"That's what I'm talking about," Katie agreed. "We all brag sometimes."

"Maybe I'll stop by that tournament after my soccer game tomorrow," Jeremy said slowly. "You know, to cheer Kevin on."

"I think I'll go, too," Becky said quickly. "I could meet you there, Jeremy. We can sit together."

Jeremy blushed.

Katie sighed. Poor Jeremy. Becky was always embarrassing him. She had a huge crush on Jeremy. But Katie knew he didn't like Becky . . . at least not *that* way.

"We should all go," Katie said.

"Not me," George insisted.

"Come on, George. He's your best friend," Katie reminded him.

"Not anymore," George told her.

"We're all going to be there," Katie told George. "If you don't go, there won't be anyone around for you to hang out with anyway."

"Fine!" George finally said. "I'll go. But only to see him lose."

"Whatever," Katie said with a sigh. "Just as long as you are there."

Chapter 8

It was hot and stuffy inside the karate gym. By the time Katie got there, a lot of her friends were already seated in the bleachers that surrounded the orangey-brown hardwood floor where the tournament was taking place.

"Here, Katie, I saved a seat for you," Emma W. shouted out. She scooted over a bit so Katie could sit between her and Jeremy.

Becky was seated on Jeremy's other side. Farther down the row were George, Andrew, and Manny.

"Sorry I'm late," Katie said. "My mom was busy talking to Mrs. Lock. I had to wait a while until she got off the phone before we could drive over here."

"I was really surprised when you told me she was getting her tonsils out," Emma told Katie. "How is she feeling?"

"Better, I guess," Katie replied. "She still can't talk, but her parents bought her a pair of purple glow-in-the-dark pajamas to wear in the hospital. That made her pretty happy."

"Hey, check it out!" Jeremy interrupted. "The grown-up black belts are putting on a show before the tournament begins."

"*KEEYAH!*" A shout rang out through the gym. A man in a karate uniform with a black belt raised up his arm slowly and then quickly brought his hand down onto a pile of cement blocks.

"That *had* to hurt," Manny said as the cement blocks crumbled in half.

But the man with the black belt didn't seem to be hurting. In fact, he was smiling proudly.

Katie and her friends watched as another

grown-up black belt stood in the center of the gym. Five other black belts stood in front of him. Each of them was holding a thick wooden board.

"*KEEYAH!*" the man shouted. He leaped up into the air. His arms were spread out wide. So were his legs. In a single movement, he managed to break two boards with his feet, two with his hands, and one with his head.

"Wow!" Andrew exclaimed. "Do you think Kevin can do something like that?"

"No way," George said.

"He's only a yellow belt," Katie reminded Andrew and George. "But maybe someday he will be able to."

George frowned, but he didn't say anything.

"Where is Kevin anyway?" Andrew asked.

Katie looked down at the group of kids in white uniforms. She spotted Kevin sitting with a group of boys and girls who, like him, had bright yellow belts tied around their waists.

"There he is," Katie said, pointing toward the yellow belts.

"He's such a big shot," George groaned. "Look how he's holding that piece of wood."

"*All* the kids are holding pieces of wood," Emma pointed out. "They need them for the tournament."

"Do you really think he can break that

wooden board with his foot?" Jeremy asked
the others.

"Yes," Katie answered.

"No," George answered at the same time.

Katie sighed. George was being a real pain.
She turned her eyes toward the gym floor, and
watched as one black belt grabbed his opponent
by the arm and flipped him upside down.

"That was so cool!" Katie exclaimed. She
stood up and began to move toward the end of
the row.

"Where are you going?" Emma asked her.

"To the phone," Katie replied. "I have to
call Suzanne. I promised to call her and fill
her in on what's going on. You know how she
hates missing anything! I can't wait to tell her
about the guy who broke the cement blocks."

"You'd better hurry up," Emma told her.
"The kids' part of the tournament is going to
begin any minute now."

"I'll be right back. I promise," Katie
answered.

Luckily, the phone booth was empty when Katie arrived. Katie opened the door to the phone booth and stepped inside.

She reached into her pocket and pulled out a quarter. But before she could put the coin in the phone, she felt a cool breeze on the back of her neck.

Katie gulped. She'd felt that breeze before. *Lots of times.*

Oh, no! That was no ordinary wind. It was the magic wind!

The phone booth was small and cramped. But that didn't stop the magic wind. It still managed to circle wildly around Katie. She gulped and shut her eyes tight as the tornado swirled around her.

And then it stopped. Just like that. The magic wind was gone.

And so was Katie Carew.

Chapter 9

"KEEYAH!"

Katie jumped and opened her eyes. Right in front of her was a big man in a white karate suit with a black belt.

"AAAAAHHHHHHH!" Katie screamed back at him. She was really scared.

The man leaped back and kicked his leg hard. He flipped around, took a running jump, and . . . *bam*! He broke a thick cement block in two.

The crowd applauded.

A boy seated near Katie on the hardwood floor looked over at her strangely. "Kevin, why did you scream like that?" he asked. "You know Mr. Thomas would never hurt you."

Kevin? Katie gulped. She looked around. She was seated with a group of boys and girls. They were all wearing karate uniforms. But Kevin was nowhere to be seen.

Still, the boy sitting next to her had definitely said, "Kevin."

Katie knew that could mean only one thing. She had become Kevin! *Right before the tournament was about to start.*

Just then, a dark-haired woman with a blue belt around her waist walked over to the group of children on the floor.

"Okay, white belts, you're up first," she told the kids. "Line up, bow to the judges, and get ready to break your pieces of wood."

Katie watched as eight kids in uniforms with white belts stood up and walked to the center of the floor. They stood before the judges in two perfectly straight rows.

Everyone's attention was on the white belts. Katie smiled. Now was the perfect time

to sneak out of the gym! She had to find a
place where she could be alone. After all, the
magic wind only came when there was nobody
else around. And Katie had to get the wind
to turn her back into herself before it was
Kevin's turn to compete in the tournament!

Quietly, Katie got on all fours and began to
crawl toward the doorway at the back of the
gym. But before she could get very far, the boy
next to her grabbed onto her yellow belt and
tugged her back.

"What are you doing?" he asked her. "You can't leave now. No one's allowed to leave the gym once the tournament has begun. That's the rule."

Katie frowned. Sometimes rules really stank.

She watched as the grown-up black belts held up pieces of wood. The white-belt kids took turns punching and kicking at them.

Some of the white belts managed to break the wood. Others couldn't do it. One little boy hit the wood with his fist. Then he grabbed his hand and started crying.

Ouch. That sure looked like it hurt.

Katie sighed. Kevin had said that breaking wood wasn't hard, *if* you knew what you were doing.

Unfortunately, Katie didn't know what she was doing at all.

This was *so* not good.

Chapter 10

Katie hoped that something—anything—would happen to keep the yellow belts from having to break their boards.

But nothing did. And a few minutes later, when the white belts were finished with their part of the competition, the woman with the blue belt walked over to the part of the gym where Katie and the karate students were sitting.

"Okay, yellow belts. It's your turn," she said. "Take your boards and line up. Don't forget to bow to the judges before you break your board."

There was no getting out of this now.

Katie was going to have to get up there and kick her foot through the big piece of wood she was carrying.

She really didn't want to do this. She just wanted to run away. But Katie couldn't do that to Kevin. He had really been looking forward to this tournament.

Katie was going to have to break that board. Somehow.

Katie watched as the first yellow belt stepped forward. She figured that if she studied what the other kids were doing, and just copied them, she'd be okay.

The first yellow belt, a girl with long brown braids, bowed to the judges. Then she handed her board to a grown-up with a black belt. The black belt held up the board so the girl could break it.

The yellow belt looked steadily at the board. *"KEEYAH!"* she shouted as she kicked hard with her left foot. The board snapped in two.

Everyone applauded.

The girl with the long brown braids bowed to the judges, and went back to sit with the other kids.

The next yellow belt stepped forward. Like the girl before him, he bowed and handed his board to a grown-up with a black belt.

He stared at the board for what seemed like a really long time. Then . . . *"KEEYAH!"* The boy with the yellow belt let out a yell. He kicked the board, hard. It broke instantly.

Everyone cheered.

Uh-oh. It was Kevin's turn now. Katie was going to have to get up there, in front of all those people, and the judges, and break the board. It didn't matter that she'd never done anything like this before.

Slowly she stood up and walked toward the judges. She bowed clumsily. Then she handed the board to a black belt, just as she had seen the other kids do.

As Katie stepped back from the board, she

caught a glimpse of her friends. They were all in the stands watching her. The pressure was really on now! Katie's hands were shaking. Her heart was pounding. She could feel beads of sweat forming on her forehead.

Just kick hard, Katie told herself. *Kick as hard as you can.*

Katie stared at the wood. Then she lifted her leg, leaped up high, and kicked hard.

"Keeyah!" she yelped.

BAM! The next thing Katie knew, she was sitting on the ground. And it wasn't her foot that hurt her. It was her rear end. Katie had completely missed the wood.

Instead, she'd gone flying through the air and landed on the hard floor.

It was a really strong leap. She'd flown pretty far. In fact, that would have been a really great long jump. Unfortunately, this wasn't a track meet. It didn't matter how far you jumped if you didn't break the board.

For a minute, there was silence in the gym. And then, suddenly, Katie heard George's loud laugh coming from the bleachers.

"Some champion," George shouted.

Oh, no! Katie had ruined everything for Kevin!

Tears began to form in her eyes. But Katie refused to let George see her cry. That would just make things worse for Kevin.

She had to get out of there!

Quickly, Katie turned and ran toward the door at the back of the gym.

Chapter 11

Katie stood alone in the lobby outside the gym. She wiped the tears from her eyes. That had been just awful. She'd been so embarrassed.

She was also amazed. Karate was hard to do. Really hard! Kevin had made it seem so easy. Of course, that was because he practiced a lot.

Now Katie understood why Kevin had to spend so much time working on his karate. He'd given up everything for it—the track team, soccer, even his best friend.

Just then, Katie felt a cool breeze blowing on the back of her neck. She knew right away that this was no ordinary wind. The magic wind was back!

Sure enough, a second later, the breeze had turned into a tornado. It circled around Katie wildly, lifting her up and spinning her around in midair.

And then it was gone. Just like that.

Katie Carew was back.

And so was Kevin. He was standing right next to her. But he had no idea how he had gotten there.

"What happened?" he asked Katie. "Why are we out here?"

"Well," Katie began nervously. How was she going to explain this?

"After the board-breaking competition," she began, "you, I mean, I . . . uh, er . . ."

"The board-breaking competition. Oh man," Kevin interrupted her with a groan. "Now I remember. I missed the board. I mean, I *think* I did. I'm not really sure. It's all kind of fuzzy."

"That's pretty much what happened," Katie told him.

Kevin shook his head. "I don't know how I could have done that. I *never* miss the board."

"Everybody makes mistakes," Katie told him.

"Not me. I'm always right on target. But not today," Kevin said sadly. "Of all days for me to mess up. Now I'll never be a champion."

"Well, you could still get a medal," Katie told him.

"They don't give you a medal for missing the board, Katie," he told her impatiently.

"I know that," Katie answered. "But there are two other events. You still can get a medal for sparring, or for doing your karate moves."

"They're called forms," Kevin said quietly.

"Okay *forms*," Katie repeated. "You know those really well. You should go back in there and show everyone."

Kevin shook his head. "No way. I'm done with karate. I quit!"

Now Katie felt really terrible. Kevin had loved karate—until she ruined it for him. She couldn't let him quit. She just couldn't.

"Kevin, you've got to go out there. And you've got to win a medal," she told him.

"Why?" Kevin asked her.

"Because you can't let George think he was right! He'll brag about it forever," Katie told him. "And being around someone who brags all the time is really awful."

Kevin blushed. "I guess I acted kind of stuck-up this week," he admitted.

Katie shrugged. "Kind of. But it's okay. You were just excited about the tournament."

"Yeah," Kevin said with a frown. "I thought I would win."

"You could still win something," Katie told him. "Besides, it's not about winning."

"Sure it is," Kevin insisted.

"No way," Katie said, shaking her head. "It's about doing something you love. It's about getting better and better at karate. Medals aren't important."

"I sure would like to have one, though," Kevin murmured.

"You're not going to get one standing here," she pointed out. "You've got to go in there and try."

Kevin nodded. "I guess you're right," he agreed. "Besides, I can't make a bigger fool out of myself than I already have."

"You won't make a fool out of yourself," Katie assured him. "You know this stuff. Just do what you've been showing us all week."

Chapter 12

"Wow, Kevin, your silver medal is huge," Jeremy said. The tournament was over, and the kids were all standing around Kevin in the gym lobby.

"It's heavy, too. You want to feel it?" Kevin asked. He lifted the medal from around his neck, and handed it to Jeremy.

"You really beat up that other yellow belt," Manny said.

"I didn't *really* beat him up," Kevin said. "That's not the point of sparring. You're just supposed to show how well you can defend yourself. I guess I did better than he did."

"Yeah, well, the guy who won the gold

medal did better than you did," George reminded him.

Katie sighed. She couldn't believe George was starting another fight.

But Kevin had had enough sparring for one day. "I guess so," he agreed with George. "But I'll get him next time."

"Yay!" Katie cheered Kevin, before George could say anything else.

"Can I try on your bronze medal?" Becky asked Kevin. "The one you got for doing your karate forms?"

"Sure," Kevin said. He lifted the other medal from around his neck. "Just don't drop it."

"I don't know what everybody's making such a big deal about," George grumbled. "It's not like this is the Olympics or anything."

"It's still pretty cool," Jeremy told him. "*You've* never won anything like this before."

George frowned.

"Yeah, but maybe he will," Kevin said. "I

71

mean, he could win a track medal, if he tries hard enough." Kevin was really trying hard to be nice.

"And if he ties his shoelace tighter," Jeremy said with a laugh.

George blushed. "I'm not letting that happen again. I'm getting Velcro sneakers for track."

"Are you going to wear your medals to school?" Andrew asked Kevin.

Kevin almost nodded. Then he looked over at Katie. He shook his head instead. "Nah. That would be like bragging. It's just good knowing I won them."

At that moment, Mrs. Camilleri walked over to where the kids were. "Do you all want to go out for ice cream to celebrate?" she asked them.

Of course everyone did. Even George. He never gave up a chance to have ice cream.

"Hey, George, will you show me how you suck the ice cream out of the bottom of the cone?" Kevin asked.

"You want *me* to teach *you* something?"

George asked. He sounded surprised.

Kevin nodded. "Every time I try it, the ice cream spills all over my shirt. You're the champion of ice-cream-cone-sucking."

George grinned. "Yeah, I guess I am. Too bad they don't give medals for that. I'd definitely get a gold medal. Or at the very least, a chocolate-chip-mint one!"

Katie giggled. It was good to see George and Kevin getting along again.

"Hey, George, do you want to practice running the relay with me at recess tomorrow?" Emma W. asked him. "Maybe you and I could try again at next week's track meet."

"Um, well, I . . ." George seemed kind of embarrassed. He and Emma didn't hang out together very much.

"That sounds like a good idea," Kevin said. "And I'll time you guys. I could be like your coach. That way, I could help the team, even though I'm not on it anymore."

"Great idea!" George said. "I'll let you use my new stopwatch."

"Cool," Kevin said.

George turned to Katie. "You want to practice, too, Katie Kazoo? You could work on your long jump."

"Sure," Katie said happily. She was so glad everybody was friends again.

$$\times \qquad \times \qquad \times$$

About a half hour later, Katie was sitting on Suzanne's bed. Suzanne was happily eating a bowl of chocolate ice cream. Mrs. Camilleri had dropped Katie off at Suzanne's house with a whole pint of it.

"So then, Kevin turned and kicked this kid really hard, right in the stomach," Katie told Suzanne. "It was a good thing they both had all this padding on. I didn't know Kevin was so strong."

He only won a silver medal, though, right? Suzanne wrote on her pad.

Katie rolled her eyes. "A silver medal is a

huge deal, Suzanne," she said. "You don't have any medals."

Suzanne shrugged.

"It's a cool medal. You should see it. It's really heavy, too. Kevin let us all try them on," Katie continued.

Suzanne looked a little sad. *You know,* she wrote, *this is the first time you knew about something before I did. I'm usually the one who knows about everything that's going on.*

Katie thought about that. It wasn't exactly true. Suzanne didn't know about the magic wind. She didn't know that Katie had turned into people like Jeremy, Lucille, Mr. Kane, and one time, even Suzanne herself.

But Katie sure wasn't going to tell her that. She couldn't! Besides, Suzanne already felt bad enough. Why let her know that there were plenty of things going on that she had no idea about?

I'll be back after I have my tonsils out. Then things will go back to normal, Suzanne wrote.

Well, sort of normal, Katie thought. *As normal as things can be when there's a magic wind around!*

Tomato Sauce

Here's the recipe for the yummy tomato sauce Katie and her friends in the cooking club cooked up. Make some yourself, and then pour it over your favorite pasta.

Make sure that you, like Katie, have a grown-up around to help with the chopping and cooking.

This recipe makes 4 servings of sauce.

You will need:
1 carrot, diced
1 medium onion, chopped
1 stalk of celery with the leaves still on, chopped

2 tablespoons of olive oil

1 clove of garlic, minced

5 basil leaves, torn

2–3 ripe medium tomatoes, skinned, drained, and chopped

Salt and pepper to taste

Here's what you do:

1. Sauté the carrot, onion, celery, and garlic in a saucepan with olive oil for about 5 minutes over medium heat.

2. Add the basil leaves and then the tomatoes. Stir.

3. Add salt and pepper to taste.

4. Simmer the sauce on low heat for about half an hour, until the sauce thickens.

5. Serve over your favorite pasta.